7/02

D1092256

James Whitcomb
RILEY
Young Poet

Written by
Minnie Belle Mitchell
&
Montrew Dunham

Illustrated by
Cathy Morrison

Patria Press, Inc.
3842 Wolf Creek Circle
Carmel, IN 46033
Phone 877-736-7930
Website: www.patriapress.com

Printed and bound in the United States of America
10 9 8 7 6 5 4 3 2 1

Text originally published by the Bobbs-Merrill Company, 1942, in the
Childhood of Famous Americans Series© The Childhood of Famous Americans
Series© is a registered trademark of Simon & Schuster, Inc.

Library of Congress Cataloging-in-Publication Data

Mitchell, Minnie Belle, 1860-1955.
    James Whitcomb Riley : young poet / written by
Minnie Belle Mitchell and Montrew Dunham ; illustrated by Cathy Morrison.
    p. cm. — (Young patriots series ; 5)
    Summary: Provides a fictional account of the childhood of the "Childrens
Poet," who wrote more than one hundred poems including "Little Orphant
Annie" and "The Old Swimmin' Hole."
    ISBN 1-882859-10-3 (hardcover) — ISBN 1-882859-11-1 (pbk.)
    1. Riley, James Whitcomb, 1849-1916—Juvenile fiction. [1. Riley, James
Whitcomb, 1849-1916—Childhood and youth—Fiction.] I. Dunham,
Montrew. II. Morrison, Cathy, ill. III. Title. IV. Series.

PZ7.M694 Jam 2002
[Fic]—dc21   2001008229

Edited by Harold Underdown
Design by Timothy Mayer at inari

Contents

Illustrations

Numerous smaller illustrations

Dedication from the original edition
by Minnie Belle Mitchell, 1942:

Dedicated to my son
John F. Mitchell Jr.

The verses from Riley's poems, which appear in some chapters,
are used with permission of his heirs and may be found in
The Complete Works of James Whitcomb Riley, published
by The Bobbs-Merrill Company, copyright 1916

Books in the Young Patriots Series

Chapter 1

Swinging High

"**H**ey, Johnty, wait for me!" Bud called as he ran after the big boys in the backyard. His big brother ran to the rope swing, which was gently blowing back and forth in the chilly spring wind. Johnty leaped onto the seat and with a push of his feet swung back and then soared into the air.

Bud laughed with joy as he watched his brother swing higher and higher and shouted,

"My turn, Johnty! Next, it's my turn!"

The boys were running and jumping all over the back lot. Bud shivered a little. The pale sun disappeared behind a dark cloud. The fresh spring air was moist, but the wind was cold. Noah climbed the cherry tree, which was covered with white blossoms. The petals were tossed in the wind as they fell to the ground. Eck ran over to the old apple tree, and he leaned back, almost like an acrobat, and jumped to get hold of a branch to lift himself up into the tree.

Ring barked and barked as he ran back and forth chasing all the boys. Bud was watching his brother Johnty swing higher and higher into the sky, and he didn't see Ring run in front of him. He tripped on Ring and fell flat on the dog. They both scrambled to their feet, and Ring danced around him barking wildly and wagging his fluffy brown tail.

Bud looked up at Johnty and shouted, "Come on . . . Johnty! It's my turn!"

Eck yelled from his perch in the apple tree, "Johnty, you might as well give him his turn. Your little brother always wants to do what you are doing."

Johnty stopped pumping. As the swing slowed down and he leaped out onto his knees on the muddy ground, he called, "Come on, Bud, if you want your turn!"

Bud ran to the swing and jumped on to the seat. He gave it a strong push with his feet, and then leaning forward and back, pumped the swing into going higher and higher. He laughed with delight as he went so high that the ropes of the swing would jerk, and it almost felt like he was going to fall off the seat! He was so high he could see clear

. . . leaning forward and back, Bud pumped the
swing into going higher and higher. . . .

over the top of their log house and even see the National Road in front of their house.

He saw Mother come out. She was going over to the apple hole to get some vegetables. He saw her look up at the darkening sky and hug her woolen shawl around her shoulders. She walked over to the barn and got a hoe to scrape the dirt from the top of the storage pit, where the vegetables were stored for use through the winter months. She looked up when she heard Bud call, "Look, Ma! I'm doin' skyscrapers!"

Mother took a deep breath when she saw how high Bud was swinging! "James Whitcomb Riley, what are you doing! You are swinging too high!" She couldn't believe he was growing up so fast. She smiled as she looked at the little boy with his soft blond hair ruffled in the wind. And she thought back to that seventh day of October in 1849, when James was born in their little log cabin.

Elizabeth and Reuben Riley, John and James' parents, had moved to the very small village of Greenfield in 1844. They had built a log cabin on the National Road like most of the other houses in the village. Reuben was a lawyer and put his sign out on his front door. He soon became very successful in town. He served as the mayor of Greenfield, and then he was elected to serve in the Indiana State Legislature. And when their second son was born, they named him James Whitcomb for Governor James Whitcomb, who was Father's friend.

Next after Johnty came
His little towhead brother, Bud by name,
And O how white his hair was—and how thick
His face with freckles,—and his ears, how quick
And curious and intrusive!—And how pale
The blue of his big eyes—

Their log cabin was small but cozy and bright. It had a big living room, a little kitchen with a huge fireplace, and a low loft upstairs. The loft had such a sloping ceiling that even Johnty and Bud bumped their heads if they weren't careful. Father had hung corn and beans from the rafters up there, and Mother had stored hard green pears among the hickory nuts and walnuts on the floor.

Their vegetables had been stored in the apple hole in the yard. In the fall Father had dug a hole and lined it with straw. Then they laid cabbages, beets, parsnips, potatoes, and apples on the straw. They covered the vegetables and apples with more straw and piled dirt on top. They left a little opening at one end, which was also covered with straw and loose dirt.

Mother was gathering some cabbages and potatoes from the apple hole when, suddenly, heavy raindrops started to fall. Then, almost at once, the rain came down in drenching sheets blowing across the yard. "Come quickly, boys!" Mother cried as she ran toward the door of the house.

She looked back as Johnty ran toward her, and the other boys ran home, but Bud was still twisting in the swing. "Bud, come on! You are going to get soaked!"

Bud had twisted again and again until the swing ropes were taut . . . and he couldn't get out until they untwisted round and round! With the rain in his face, round and round he went until finally the swing slowed and he hopped off. He was so dizzy he had trouble running to the house!

Mother held the door and led both boys over to the fireplace hearth to dry. They stood before the open fire, their wet clothes dripping. They rubbed their cold wet hands and stamped their feet as they dried off. They leaned over to see the kettles and pots hanging on their heavy iron hooks in the fireplace and the hearth oven. Mother had supper almost ready, and there were so many good smells. Mother was a wonderful cook of honey cakes and roasts and puddings and everything else.

Mother said, "Stand back boys, I need to tend my cooking."

Johnty and Bud climbed up on the benches at the table in the kitchen so they could watch their mother preparing supper. With a heavy potholder, Mother adjusted the crane, swinging the kettle out of the fire and more over the hearth. Hungrily, they watched as Mother moved the kettles and pots to just the right place, and then she took the bread out of the hearth oven. It smelled so good!

"Can we eat?" Johnty asked.

Bud nodded his head. "We're very hungry." He could almost taste that good bread.

Mother smiled, "I know you are. . . . It won't be long. We'll eat as soon as your father comes."

"Then tell us a story while we wait!"

"There is only time for a teensy one," Mother said. Then she began, "Do you see the lid jiggling on the kettle?"

Bud nodded. He could see the heavy iron lid dancing up and down on the kettle.

Mother went on, "There are little fairies that live in the red-hot embers in the fireplace. Every now and then they like to jump up onto the lid. They dance jigs and cut all kinds of capers. Do you hear their feet tapping away there?"

Bud sat with his chin propped on his hands as he watched the lids intently. He listened carefully. Then he heard. He could hear the fairy feet tapping.

"Inside the kettle there are other fairies—imps, really. They hear the little coal fairies and plan tricks." Mother said softly. "Do you hear them chuckling and whispering? They like to push up on the lid all together. Then what will happen?"

"The imps will spill the coal fairies into the fire," laughed Johnty.

Bud frowned, "That isn't very nice of the imps."

"It's all in fun, Bud. Remember that the coal fairies live and play in the hot embers of the fire," Mother said.

After that Bud watched carefully to see if the fairies could hold the lid down. When the lid tilted, Bud shouted, "The imps are winning! The imps are winning! Hold on tight, little coal fairies!" He got so excited that Mother lifted the lid off carefully and told the fairies to jump off and run home.

Chapter 2

Old Swimming Hole

On Saturday morning, when the baking had to be done, Johnty and Bud played farther from the house. "When the dinner bell on the Guymon House rings," Mother said, "you will know it is time to come home for lunch."

The boys ran home when they heard the bell ringing loud and clear. As they reached the back yard they started to march with their bare feet on the path. Bud led the line of boys as they marched into the house. They sang in loud voices:

"Pig tail done—
Go tell son,
Dinner's ready,
Pig tail done!"

Mrs. Riley laughed. "Where did you learn that funny song? I've never heard it before."

"Bud made it up," said Johnty.

And Eck added, "He's always making up funny songs and rhymes like that." Johnty's friends liked Bud's little jingles. They asked for new ones all the time.

After lunch Bud, Johnty, and Johnty's friends all gathered in Riley's back lot. Bud ran to the apple tree and climbed up to sit on a bottom branch.

"Hey, let's go swimming!" Eck called

"All right!" The boys shouted and started to run to the old swimmin' hole.

The weather was perfect for swimming. The afternoon sun was beating down relentlessly. Old Sorrell stood in his hot stall, flicking his tail back and forth to shoo away the flies. Ring lay on the bare ground under the apple tree, panting with the heat. Bud, up in the apple tree under the green leaves, was a little cooler, but he quickly scrambled down from his perch and ran to catch up with the big boys.

When Johnty saw his little brother, he stopped for a moment and called back, "You stay home, Bud. You are too little to go with us today. We're going to Brandywine Creek. You can't swim, and you might fall in and drown!"

"I can too swim!" Bud retorted.

Johnty shook his head and replied patiently, "Oh, Bud, you are too little. You don't know how to swim!"

Bud stuck out his lower lip stubbornly, as he insisted, "Can, too!" And he followed close behind the boys as they walked down the dirt path to the creek.

"Oh, let him come," Noah said, "We'll watch him, Johnty." The boys liked to have Bud with them. He was always fun.

Happily Bud followed the boys on the path under the shade of the big forest trees and through the underbrush and weeds towering above his head. The dust under his bare feet was soft as velvet.

Brandywine Creek was a pretty stream that flowed through the woods only a short distance from the Riley home. Willow trees and sycamores grew along its banks. No matter how hot and sticky it was anywhere else, it was always cool and shady at the creek. Little children played in the shallow spots and the older children swam in the deep pools.

*Oh! The old swimmin' hole! In the happy
    days of yore,
When I ust to lean above it on the old
    sickamore. . . . .*

Thare the bullrushes growed, and the cattails
  So tall,
And the sunshine and shadder fell over it all.

Bud liked watching the boys dive off the log that lay across the stream. And then he watched eagerly as they held on to a root at the bottom to see how long before they came up. He cheered excitedly and clapped his hands.

However, after a while, he grew tired of just watching. He wanted to swim, too. So he ran out on the log and jumped in. He hit the water with a splash! And right after him so did Eck and Noah! They pulled him out on the bank in a hurry.

But when Bud jumped in again, Johnty decided it was time for Bud to go home. He dragged Bud into the house, and said, "Here, Mother, you keep Bud with you. He won't stay out of the deep water."

"I can swim," Bud protested.

"No, he can't," Johnty said disgustedly. "We keep having to pull him out!"

Mr. Riley was working at his desk and heard them talking. "Bud, you're too little to swim."

"I'm going to swim," insisted Bud as he ran across the back lot and down the path toward the creek.

Father got up from his desk and said, "If he is

Bud liked watching the boys dive off the log
that lay across the stream.

going to run off to the creek, he had better know
how to swim."

"Oh, he is much too small," Mother said. "He'll
step into a deep hole and drown!"

"He needs to learn how to swim," said Father.
He called after Bud, "Wait for me. I'll teach you to
swim."

Bud shouted triumphantly, "Father is going to
teach me to swim!"

When the boys saw Mr. Riley, they clambered

13

out onto the bank. They all grinned. The big boys knew there was only one way to learn to swim. They gathered around to see how Bud would like it.

Mr. Riley took Bud to the bank above the deep pool. "Ready?" he asked.

"Ready!" shrieked Bud with delight. "In you go, then," said his father as he tossed him into the water. "Now swim out!" he shouted.

But Bud didn't swim out!

Chapter 3

Father's Surprise

Bud's father and the boys looked expectantly at the ripples where Bud went in as they waited for him to come to the surface. Anxiously they waited and waited for him to come up. The water smoothed and nothing happened. Mr. Riley leaped into the water with all his clothes on. Johnty could not wait any longer, and he dived in too, with Noah right behind him! They swam underwater trying to see Bud, and when they came up for air, there was Bud sitting on the bank.

He looked at his father in surprise as he said, "Father, your clothes are all wet!"

His father picked Bud up in his arms. He was so relieved to see him safe and sound.

"Where were you? What happened to you, Bud?" asked Mr. Riley.

"I held on to the root, just like Johnty," Bud answered. "See!" and he jumped in again before his father could stop him. Bud went down to the bottom of the swimmin' hole. He grabbed onto the root and held on just as he had seen the others do. When he came up, he splashed around as lively as a duck.

Father took a deep breath as he watched Bud dog-paddle over to the bank and pull himself out of the water.

"See, I can swim just like everybody else!" Bud shouted.

Father laughed, "You sure can! I guess there's no reason why you can't come to the ole swimmin' hole with the boys anytime you want to!"

After that Bud went with the boys to Brandywine creek often that summer, but he also spent a lot of time sitting out by the front fence. He liked to watch the people, animals, and carts passing through Greenfield on the National Road. He saw wagons and oxcarts, buggies, and coaches carrying the mail, all rolling along on the smooth planks of the National Road. There were the pioneer families going West in their big Connestoga wagons. Bud watched and wondered how it would be to live in a big wagon and not even know where your new home would be. Bud didn't even want to move into their new house, which was just in front of their log cabin. And that was in the same place in the same town!

He looked back at their new house, which was almost finished. He felt strange about going to live in another house. He worried that it wouldn't feel like home. Their log house was just right, with the big kitchen where Mother did all the cooking, and the long table where they all sat to eat. The big front room was warm and cozy with its large fireplace, where in the cold weather, the fire crackled and glowed with friendly warmth. In one corner was the big high bed with the trundle bed underneath where he slept. Father's big double desk was in the other corner where he worked with all his law books. Then Bud thought about the upstairs loft. On rainy days he and Johnty stretched out on the floor and listened to the sounds of the rain pelting on the roof.

But Father said they needed a bigger house, and all summer Father and his helpers had worked building the white frame house. Though Father was a busy lawyer who spent most of his days at the county courthouse, he liked to work in his shop making furniture and cupboards for the new house. He was also shaping and building the black walnut stairs and staircase for the front hall in their new house.

Bud ran to the workshop to find his father. The old woodhouse was cool and dark. He walked in past the neatly stacked firewood, to the other half of the shed that was Father's workshop. Though he didn't hear his father at work, he called anyway. "Pa, are you here?"

There was only silence. Bud was disappointed. He loved to watch his father at work as he carefully smoothed and planed the wood to make the handrail for the staircase and the doors for the cupboards. He especially liked when Father planed off satiny curls of fresh thin woodshavings. The boys would pick them off the floor and play with the fragrant loops of wood.

Slowly Bud walked back out into the bright sunshine. The rope swing dangling from the tree looked inviting, but he decided to go out front by the road. He wandered out to the front fence where he just stood and thought and watched the traffic on the road.

He was leaning on the front gate, gently swinging when he heard his mother call. "Bud, come in. . . . your father has something for you!" He ran to the front door and was surprised when he saw his father standing in the kitchen with a package on the table.

"Your father has something special for you. Come and see what it is," Mother said.

Bud hurried to the table and opened the box. His eyes opened wide as he stood and stared.

Bud put the suit on. It fit perfectly.

Inside the box he saw long pants, a vest with a buckle, and a coat. The suit was made exactly like the one his father wore!

"For me?" Bud asked. He could hardly talk.

Mother nodded. "Put it on. Let's see how your new suit fits." Bud put the suit on. It fit perfectly.

"Splendid, you look just like the judge!" Father exclaimed. "Come, we're going down to the courthouse."

Bud walked proudly with his father as they went down to the courthouse. Court was in session when they walked in to the dark room. The judge was sitting at the bench and peering down at the lawyers who were arguing a case.

Reuben Riley and his young son stood quietly at the back of the room until that case was finished, and the lawyers and their clients had walked out of the room. Then Mr. Riley stepped forward and introduced his young son in his grown-up suit, "Gentlemen of the Court, may I present Judge Riley!"

Bud felt a little embarrassed, but he soon started to enjoy all the attention. Then Judge Wick leaned over his bench to shake the hand of "Judge Riley." When the lawyers and the clerks called him Judge Riley, Bud started to imitate the real judge. And everyone laughed.

Chapter 4

Bud Goes to School

The Rileys moved into their new home in 1854, and it didn't take long for five-year-old Bud to feel right at home. Father had the old log house moved to the back of the house to be the kitchen. There was a comfortable parlor with a fine fireplace, which had built-in cupboards on each side from the floor to the ceiling. Father had made these cupboards in his wood shop from beautiful black walnut. They were called presses. All the jams, jellies, and canned fruit were kept in there to keep them from freezing in the wintertime.

Behind the parlor was the big dining room, and across the hall from the parlor was Father's office, where Father had his big double desk. The top part of the desk was made of shelves for his law books.

Father had also made the steep curving staircase in the front hall, which led to the upstairs bedrooms. Upstairs there was a big room where Johnty slept, just behind Mother and Father's bedroom. And there was a cot in Johnty's room for Bud when he was big enough to move out of the trundle bed.

Bud still slept in the trundle bed just as he had in the log house. The trundle bed was a low child's bed, which was under the big bed by day. At night it rolled out, or was "trundled" out into the room. Bud liked his trundle bed, but he would be glad when Mother thought he was old enough to sleep in the cot in the room with Johnty.

O the old trundle-bed! O the old trundle-bed!
With its plump little pillow, and old-fashioned
*   spread;*
Its snowy white sheets, and the blankets above,
Smoothed down and tucked round with the
*   touches of love . . .*

Mother had a hired girl who helped her with all the work in their new house. The hired girl's name was Floretty, and when she was busy in the kitchen, she pretended to be as cross as an old witch, but she didn't fool anybody. Johnty and Bud loved her. They knew the harder she scolded, the bigger the cookies would be.

Mr. Riley had a helper too. Johnty called him the Raggedy Man, so everybody else did. Bud and

Johnty were always at his heels. They kept him busy mending their toys, fixing their hurts, and telling them stories. He hardly had time to get anything else done.

One evening Father said, "Bud, my boy, you are now past five years old. You should be going to school."

"I don't need to go to school. I can read," said Bud. "I'll show you." He climbed up on a chair and took down a big book from his father's bookshelf. He read a whole poem out of it.

"That's remarkable," said Mr. Riley.

Bud's mother smiled. "He thinks he is reading it," she said, "but he is just repeating what he knows by heart. I have read the poems in that book to him many times."

Bud started school anyway. The first morning he pleaded with his mother to let him stay home. "I don't want to leave you here alone," he said. His blue eyes filled with tears.

His mother smiled and put the primer book in his hand, "Run along now, dear. Old Ring will keep me company."

Bud's first school was like a kindergarten. Only young children attended Mrs. Neill's school, which she held in her own little house. There were about twelve children in her school. Bud had always known Mrs. Neill and liked her, but he didn't want to have to stay indoors all day.

On the way to school he was too unhappy to notice how cool and shady Main Street was under the locust trees. He scuffed at the pebbles in the gravel walk that led to Mrs. Neill's house.

As he walked he was thinking, "My father knows a lot more than any old school does." He thought about going out to the farm with his father, who taught him all about growing crops and about the trees in the forest and the animals and the birds. He frowned a little and shook his head, and then he thought about his mother, and he said to himself defiantly, "She can tell better stories . . . and make up poems . . . better than in any old book!"

Bud stopped at the front gate. He thought maybe he should run away. "I could just follow the old National Road over the hill and never go to school ever!"

But before he could start, Ed Howard, one of his friends, saw him and called, "Bud Riley is here, teacher!"

"So he is," said Mrs. Neill and led him into the schoolroom.

The children sat on low benches placed against the wall. Many of Bud's playmates were there. He sat next to Willie Pierson and felt a little better about having to go to school.

After a while Mrs. Neill asked the Primer Class to stand up. These were children who had been to school before.

"Ed," the teacher said, "you may read the lessons about the cow."

Bud felt sorry when Ed didn't know a single word.

Willie was next, but he only knew a few words, and he stumbled through trying to read and couldn't.

Bud opened his primer and said "Don't feel bad, Mrs. Neill. I'll read it for you." Bud read the story straight through without having to stop for any word he didn't know. He did know how to read, after all!

Bud didn't understand why he had to go to school. He didn't like the next day at school any more than the first day. He didn't like the spelling lesson in the morning or reading in the primer in the afternoon. His eyelids grew heavy as he stared out of the window and listened to the hum of the bees. The children's voices made him drowsy. All at once he fell asleep and slumped over his desk.

Mrs. Neill did not try to wake him. Gently she lifted him and carried him to a pallet on the floor

The children sat on low benches placed against the wall.

in the front room. She kept these pallets ready for the younger children to nap. The other children didn't laugh. They were used to seeing children take afternoon naps at school.

As soon as Mrs. Neill laid Bud down, he woke

up. He pretended he was asleep until she left. Then he sat up and looked around. There was an old man asleep in a rocking chair by the window. He was snoring. His lips puffed out and sucked in when he snored. Bud sat there and imitated him.

Soon he heard footsteps. He lay down and closed his eyes again. In came Mrs. Neill with Willie Pierson in her arms, and she laid him beside Bud. As soon as the teacher was gone, Willie sat up. Bud poked him in the ribs. They began to giggle. Mrs. Neill looked in, but they pretended to be sound asleep.

When Mrs. Neill went back to the classroom, Bud pulled a rocking chair over to the window. He leaned back and folded his hands across his stomach and began to rock and snore just like the old gentleman.

Poor Willie laughed out loud. Bud frowned and looked at Willie. He wasn't trying to be funny. He just wanted to see if he could snore like the old man. Bud was sorry that Willie had laughed because Mrs. Neill had heard and now they had to go back to the schoolroom.

Though the days passed, Bud was still restless in school. Mrs. Neill often allowed him to go get a drink. Sometimes she took him to the kitchen and gave him a cookie. Or she let him pass around the room with a small bucket of cool water and give each one of the children a drink from the gourd dipper.

He was too active, too full of fun, to be quiet very long. He liked the woods and creek best. As long as he was free to be outdoors, Bud was happy.

Best, I guess,
Was the old Recess—
No tedious lessons nor irksome rule—
When the whole round world was as sweet to me
As the big ripe apple I brought to School.

Chapter 5

Noey Bixler's Snowman

Reuben Riley often went on business to Indianapolis. It was a long trip on horseback or with horse and buggy, and usually he wouldn't get back until late at night. Sometimes he would take the spring wagon so that he could bring home provisions. Bud and Johnty were glad when their father took a trip to the city because he always brought back gifts to their mother and to each of them.

One night when Mr. Riley returned from Indianapolis, everyone rushed out to greet him. The spring wagon was loaded with gifts.They were all eager to help unload the bundles. First, the larger pieces were unwrapped. There was a set of beautiful chairs with upholstered seats for mother. Then gifts were pulled out for Johnty and for Floretty and the hired man.

Bud waited patiently for his gift, but the wagon was empty! His heart fell! He tried hard not to cry as he asked sadly, "Father, didn't you bring anything for me?"

Father smiled mysteriously as he reached under the seat of the spring wagon. He drew out a package and gave it to Bud. "Of course, I brought you something."

Bud opened the package as fast as he could. When he saw it was crayons and a sketchbook, he cried, "Oh Father, thank you!"

> *Parunts don't git toys an' things,*
>   *Like you'd think they ruther.—*
> *Mighty funny Chris'mus gif's*
>   *Parunts gives each other!*
> *Pa give Ma a barrel o' flour,*
>   *An' Ma she give to Pa*
> *The nicest dinin'-table*
>   *She know he ever saw!*

Bud was so glad to have the crayons and the sketchbook. The first thing he did was to make a valentine for his mother. He wrote a little poem and then he drew a picture to go with the poem. Mother was delighted with Bud's valentine and gave him three big cookies. Bud could tell by the warm smile on his mother's face that she was pleased.

The sun was bright, but the days were cold as

Bud trudged to school. One day when it seemed winter should be nearly over, suddenly heavy flakes of snow began to fall. Bud couldn't keep his thoughts on his lessons as he watched the swirling snow through the schoolroom window. The wind howled, and the air was drenched with the falling snow. "Look, Mrs. Neill, it's a blizzard!" Bud exclaimed.

Mrs. Neill interrupted her lesson and went to look out the door. When she opened the schoolroom door, waves of wet snow blew in across the floor. Quickly she shut the door and said, "You are right, Bud. I think you all need to start home."

Bud grabbed his coat from the hook and pulled his hat down over his ears. All the boys and girls ran out into the fierce storm. The snow was piling up in great mounds around the fence posts. They ran with the wind in their faces, and the snow clung to their hats and coats. The snow landed on his eyelashes, and he narrowed his eyes so that he could see.

All the children ran and played in the snow. Bud lay down on the blanket of snow and waved his arms and legs back and forth to make a butterfly. Some of the girls made angels.

The boys rolled big, soft snowballs and lobbed them at each other. Bud dived into a snowbank, and the big boys had to pull him out. He had such a good time that he didn't even know that his clothes were soaking wet from the snow. The bitter wind sweeping across the fields was so cold that it froze Bud's clothes into a coat of ice.

Suddenly he realized how cold he was. He was so cold that he shivered and shook, and his fingers tingled. When he got home, he was so cold that his teeth were chattering.

His mother wrapped him in a warm blanket and put his feet in hot water. She gave him hot herb tea, but he was still freezing cold, and he couldn't stop shaking.

When his father came home, he felt Bud's head. Though his forehead was very hot, Bud still shivered. Father turned to Mother and said, "I think I had better go for the doctor."

When Dr. Lot Edwards came, he looked very serious as he said, "This is a very sick boy."

Bud had to stay in bed for a very long time. Grandmother Riley lived in a little house nearby, and she came to see him often. Mother would prop Bud up with pillows, and Grandmother would read to him. Sometimes they would just talk.

Bud asked Granny about when his father, Reuben, was a little boy. "How many brothers did he have? Eight?"

Grandmother's face crinkled up as she smiled and answered, "No, Reuben has seven brothers, but I have eight sons!"

"I know Uncle Mart, but who are your other sons?"

"They are all your uncles, John and Jim and George and Andy and Frank and Joe. Then I have one daughter, Sara."

"And she's not my uncle, because she's my aunt!"

Granny and Bud both laughed.

Granny pulled her shawl around her shoulders, picked up her book, and said, "Shall I read to you now?"

"Oh yes," said Bud.

Granny loved to read, and Bud loved to have her read to him. He thought she knew more about history than anybody. After she left he picked up her book and tried to read it.

He said to his mother, "Granny has read all kind of books that tell all about the land and sea and all the countries all over the world. She knows just about everything!" Mother nodded her head in agreement.

Just to look at his pretty mother made Bud feel good. Her silky blond hair framed her smooth, fair face, and her smile was always so kind and sweet.

Mother brought her mending and sat next to Bud's trundle bed while he was getting well. Bud would read to her or make up stories and poems.

Mother asked, "How do you know how to make up poems?"

"They just come to me out of the air. I hear poems in my head all the time."

"Then you must listen to them," Mother said, "and write them down."

Finally, Bud recovered enough that he could sit at the window and look out. He was lonesome for his friends. He watched the other children throwing snowballs and making forts. He wished he could be outside with them. His friends were busy playing and soon forgot how long the days seemed to this restless little boy. But Noey Bixler didn't forget.

Noey Bixler was older than Bud. Everybody liked Noey. He could make 'most anything. He made a beautiful footstool for Mrs. Riley, sleds for the boys, cages for his pets, and even wheelbarrows and ax handles for the men.

Now he made something for Bud—an enormous snowman outside Bud's window.

All the children came to watch. He made the snowman like a giant soldier standing guard. He put a gun on his shoulder and a hat on his head.

He made the snowman like a giant
soldier standing guard.

He used walnuts for the snowman's eyes and stuffing from a buggy seat for a beard.

Everyday Bud scraped the frost off the window so that he could see the snowman. His friends came each day, too. They waved at Bud and threw snowballs at his window.

When the snow began to melt around the snowman, he stood strong as ever. It was as if he were waiting for Bud to come outside.

At last when Bud was well enough to go out, he ran to the snowman and reached his arms around him as far as they would go. "I love you, old snowman, that Noey Bixler made!"

Ho, the old Snow-Man
That Noey Bixler made
He looked fierce and sassy
As a soldier on parade!

Chapter 6

Playing Store

Bud was delighted when summer came and school was over. Bud was no longer the youngest in the family now. Johnty and Bud had a new little sister, Elva May. Uncle Mart, Father's youngest brother, lived at their house most of the time, and Bud moved out of the trundle bed into his very own cot. What a happy time in their new white house with the green shutters!

The long room at the back of the house behind Mother and Father's bedroom held Johnty's bed and Uncle Mart's bed and now Bud's bed, too. On the wall at the foot of Bud's bed was a small door to the rafter room storage space. Bud wondered if there were goblins who lived in there. Gingerly, Johnty and Bud would open the door just a little and peek in. It was very dark, but there were two holes at the very end, and they wondered if that was where the goblins came in and out.

Bud and Johnty loved it when it rained at night. They would lie in bed and listen to the rain pattering on the roof. It was like when they used to lie in the loft of the log house and listen to the rain. Sometimes, though, when a strong wind was blowing, a spooky howling would come from behind that little door. Bud whispered, "Johnty, what do you think that is?"

"What do you mean?"

"That howling noise," Bud whispered. If there were goblins, he didn't want them to hear him.

Johnty took a deep breath as he answered, "I think it is just the wind," and he hoped he was right.

Just then Uncle Mart came running up the back stairs to go to bed. Both Bud and Johnty jumped upright in bed, until they saw who it was. Uncle Mart laughed when he saw Bud's wide blue eyes and his white face!

And then Bud and Johnty laughed too.

"What were you scared of?" Uncle Mart asked.

"Listen," Bud whispered, "Can you hear something in the rafter room?' And he leaned forward on his cot toward the door at the foot of his bed.

Uncle Mart listened, and then he said reassuringly, "That's just the wind blowing through the cracks. Lie down, and I'll read a story to you from my new book." He sat down on the edge of Bud's cot, and Johnty perched on the foot of the cot to listen. Bud leaned against the wall by the door into the rafter room. He took a quick glance over his shoulder at the door, but he settled back as Uncle Mart took his big book of **Tanglewood Tales** by Nathaniel Hawthorne and started to read. Uncle Mart often told them stories and read to them

Bud and Johnty were so glad when Uncle Mart was at their house. He was their youngest uncle, and he seemed just like one of the boys. He was the one who had hung their swing in the locust tree, and he built a playhouse in a big old tree where Bud and Johnty played nearly every day.

Bud loved to sit up in the playhouse. He liked to read a book, or sometimes he just thought about the stories Uncle Mart had read. The sun was warm, and the leaves of the trees rustled in the soft summer breeze. Suddenly he heard someone calling him, "Bud! . . . Hey, Bud!"

He stretched out on his stomach to look down over the edge of the playhouse. There was Ed Howard yelling up at him, "Bud, come on down! Let's play store."

Bud scrambled down from the tree, and he and Ed made their plans for the greatest store they had ever had.

First, they built a shelf against their barn to hold glasses and jars and other things. Then they made a counter and a bench for the customers to sit on.

Ed got some maple sugar candy from his house to sell, and Bud ran into his mother's kitchen and got some cinnamon cookies. Floretty called after him as he started out with a plate full of cookies, "Where are you going with those cookies?"

Bud called back to her, "We're going to sell them in our store!"

Floretty just shook her head, and thought to herself that she had just better make some more.

Bud and Ed thought of two new things to sell— soda water and "shore-nuff" store crackers. Ed's grandmother, Mrs. Gooding, gave Ed the crackers from her cracker barrel at her boarding house.

Johnty painted a big sign over the counter for them, which said, "RILEY & HOWARD STORE." Their playmates were their customers, who paid with marbles, jelly biscuits, or eggs. Ed and Bud liked to get eggs because they could trade those at the real store for "boughten" candy. When the store was ready to open, their friends all lined up. They all wanted to try the crackers and soda water.

Bud was an expert at mixing soda water. All the children liked it. He filled a glass with sugared

When the store was ready to open, their
friends all lined up.

water and a little vinegar. Then he stirred in a
pinch of soda. "Drink it while it fizzes," Bud told
his customers. It was exciting to see it fizz.

The kids would giggle when the fizz tickled
their noses as they drank the soda water. Almost
everyone thought it was a great drink, but every
now and then one would wrinkle up his face. Then

Bud knew he had put in too much soda.

They had a good store, only Bud liked the soda water and the crackers as much as the paying customers did. One day Ed was late because he had some chores to do at home. When he got to the store, there were no customers. All the crackers were gone, and there was no soda water. Bud had eaten everything!

Ed was angry. He picked up his cracker jar and drinking glasses and stormed off.

After Ed left, Bud just sat on the bench. His stomach did not feel too well. Then he decided that he needed to go see Ed and make up. He told Ed he was sorry, but he said he thought their customers wanted to buy other things besides crackers and soda water. "We ought to have red drops and licorice."

"They cost real money," grumbled Ed. He was still angry. "How could we pay for them?"

"Remember when we caught those fish in Brandywine Creek?"

"What does that have to do with red drops and licorice?"

"Remember Mrs. Gooding paid us real money for them?"

Ed frowned as he tried to remember; then he said, "She did pay us, didn't she?"

"Well, why can't we sell her some more fish right now?"

"Because we aren't good fisherman," Ed replied. "We laugh too much."

That was true. Bud and Ed sat on the front step and thought a while.

"I know!" shouted Bud triumphantly. "We can hire Johnty and his friends to fish for us."

Ed frowned again. "How can we pay them?"

"Oh, easy enough," Bud replied quickly. "We'll pay them with crackers."

The plan worked fine, and in no time at all, the store started getting piles of fish. The older boys got one cracker for every two fish, and Bud and Ed wore a path carrying the fish to Mrs. Gooding's boardinghouse.

Mrs. Gooding patted Bud and Ed on the head and said, "Good work!"

Perhaps she wondered how two small boys could catch so many fish. Perhaps she connected her empty cracker barrel with the fish, but whatever she thought, she didn't say a word.

Johnty's friends kept Bud and Ed supplied with fish. Mrs. Gooding kept the boys supplied with crackers, red drops and licorice, and the Riley & Howard Store did a brisk business.

Chapter 7

Fourth of July

The early sunshine came in through the east dormer window and fell in a golden ray across the bare floor. Bud opened his eyes slowly and looked at Johnty's bed on the other side of the room. "Are you awake, Johnty?"

"Yes, I'm up and all dressed!"

Bud was surprised to see Johnty all dressed and going toward the back stairs. He squinted his eyes together as he thought. He had such a good feeling inside, all excited and happy, and he wasn't sure why. Then suddenly he remembered. He leaped from his bed and shouted, "It's the Fourth of July!"

Johnty laughed. "And you'd better hurry," he called as he ran down the backstairs to the kitchen.

Bud dressed as fast as he could and ran downstairs to catch up with Johnty. As he burst into the kitchen, he announced loudly, "It's the Fourth of July!"

"As if I didn't know," sniffed Floretty, the hired girl, as she took custard pies from the oven. "You stop prancing around in here, or my cakes will fall flatter than fritters. Clear out of here!"

Bud peeked into the kettles bubbling on the stove. The good smells that came from under the dancing lids made his mouth water. "Wow!" he cried. "Sweet potatoes, beans, beets, greens, and chicken!"

Then he spied the pudding on the window sill. Quick as a wink, he scooped a fingerful into his mouth. And then he let out a howl, as his tongue burned from the hot pudding, "Ouch! That's hot!"

The hired girl whirled around. "Scat!" she scolded, flapping her apron at him. "How do you expect me to get the dinner ready with you eating it before I can get it off the stove?" Floretty chased him out into the garden. "Now you stay out till I call you to breakfast!"

Bud felt so good he turned handsprings and cartwheels all the way to the barn, with Ring running after him. And it was with a cartwheel he ran right into the Raggedy Man, who was coming around the corner carrying a milk bucket in one hand and a milking stool in the other! Bud sprawled on his face, and the stool went flying! Luckily the Raggedy Man managed to hang on to the bucket, although some of the milk splashed out.

Ring skidded to a stop and ran back to where Bud was scrambling to his feet. Bud said quickly, "Oh, I'm sorry. . . . I didn't see you!"

The Raggedy Man smiled a crooked smile, that turned down at the corners, almost like a frown. He said quietly, "You'd see better if you were right side up. But there's no harm done. Now I've got to get on with my chores."

"I'll help," Bud said eagerly.

The Raggedy Man smiled again but only to himself. He wasn't sure how much help Bud was going to be. He tossed the hay down for old Sorrell and the other horses. He filled the bran box and swept out the stalls. While the Raggedy Man worked, Bud talked.

"Have you seen the platform the men built in Pierson's Grove?"

The Raggedy Man shook his head.

"It's the biggest platform they ever built! Do you know why? Because this is going to be the biggest Fourth of July we ever had! There's going to be an important visitor coming from Indianapolis. His name is Professor Horatio Palmer Clarke, and he's going to make a speech this afternoon!"

Bud went on, "Father's going to meet him at the train, and he's going to drive our new carriage." He took a deep breath. "And the band is going to march in front in their new uniforms. Mother and all the ladies have been making them. There's braid on the front, and they all have new matching caps."

"My, oh my!" said the Raggedy Man. "Sounds to me like somebody's pretty excited. What are you going to do out there at Pierson's Grove?"

"I'm going to eat. Only, I have to say a poem first. Mother said if I don't make any mistakes, I can stay up past my bedtime and see the torchlight parade tonight."

Bud could hardly wait to see the torchlight parade. The streets would be very dark. There were no lights on the streets, and the big trees would block the moon and the stars. He had never seen a torchlight parade. He knew that everyone would be carrying torches made of tincans filled with lard oil and stuck on the end of short poles. Everybody would need to wear oilcloth capes and hats for protection against hot dripping oil.

Bud could have talked all morning, but soon the hired girl called him for breakfast. When he went in, Johnty was already at the table eating his breakfast. After they finished, they went with the older boys to Pierson's Grove, where they gathered wood for a big bonfire for the night meeting.

During the morning, crowds of people came into town. They came on horseback, on foot, and in wagons. The women brought baskets of food, which they had been preparing for days. They had fried chicken, ham, pork, and all kinds of pies, jellies, preserves and cakes. Every year, after the speeches on the Fourth of July, the women spread out the food, and everyone picnicked together.

Bud and Johnty went down to the station to wait for the train long before it was due. They saw many bands from other small towns, but only the Greenfield Band had matching caps and a horn player. The others had just drums and fifes.

The boys saw Father drive to the station in his carriage to meet Professor Clarke. People cheered as he passed by. Finally the train roared into town. When the speaker got off, Father went up to the steps and shook hands with him. The crowd waved and clapped. Bud was so proud and excited.

The saxhorn band led the way to the grove. Father and the visitor came next in Father's carriage, and Bud and Johnty and their friends came running along behind. The people and the bands from the other small towns followed.

The boys thought the stranger looked elegant. "Look at his stovepipe hat!" said Almon Keefer excitedly.

"Look at his coat," spoke up Willie. "Is he a preacher? I thought only preachers wore long-tailed coats."

"Did you see his watch chain?" exclaimed Johnty. "I bet it's pure gold!"

Bud noticed the man's cane and its handle of polished silver. He ran alongside the carriage for a little way to look at it again.

When the procession reached Pierson's Grove, Bud's father and the guest speaker, along with other important grown-ups, went up onto the platform. The boys sat down on the ground right in front of them.

Father stood to introduce the speaker. "It is my pleasure to present our distinguished guest, Professor Horatio Palmer Clarke."

"Do you think he will talk long?" whispered Ed.

"I'm getting awful hungry," sighed Willie.

"I'll bet there are a million cakes over there," said Eck, as he looked longingly at the food the women had started to set out.

Bud didn't care about the food. He was watching the speaker. He thought he was the most wonderful speechmaker that there ever was. He liked the way the speaker shouted until he was red in the face. He liked the way the man's coattails stood out behind him as he swung around. He liked the way he leaned far over the edge of the platform. One time he looked like he was going to fall right off the platform. Most of all he liked the way the man used his silver-headed cane. He shook it, beat the air with it, and whirled it about his head till it whistled in the wind.

All at once the speaker paused! His voice dropped as he said softly, "I have only one more word to add. I will end my remarks with a poem." Everyone leaned forward to hear. Then he started to recite. Startled, Bud looked around for his mother. The man was reciting the poem Bud had memorized.

Right in the middle of a line the speaker stopped. He mopped his forehead, looked at his watch, and started the line again. He stopped at the same place. Bud knew that the man couldn't remember what came next. Bud wanted to help him. He stood up and went to the edge of the platform and stood as tall as he could to whisper the line to him. The speaker was looking up into space as he was trying to remember and he didn't see Bud.

Suddenly Bud thought, "I can recite the poem for him!" and he pulled himself up onto the stage. He ran to the speaker, and taking his cane, said "I know the poem. I'll do it for you."

Bud did his very best. He leaned over the edge of the platform. He whirled around and he made that cane whistle. He didn't know why people laughed. He tried as hard as he could to recite the poem in exactly the same way as the guest speaker had been saying it. But the harder Bud tried, the more people laughed. At the end, he sucked in his breath until he was about to burst, and then held it to make his face red like the speaker's. He pretended to take out his handkerchief and mop his head. Then he bowed.

As he stood up from his bow, he knew something was wrong. He saw the disappointment on his mother's face, and then he turned to look at his father behind him. Father looked very grim.

Then Bud realized that everyone thought he was making fun of the speaker, and he felt like crying. He had just tried to help him by saying the poem in his place. He hopped down from the platform and ran to his mother. On the way he heard one woman say, "If that was my boy, he would be on the way to the woodshed! Mrs. Riley is too easy on that young one!"

Bud ran to his mother. She looked so troubled, as she asked, "Why did you do that?"

"Why, Mother, I had to. He forgot the poem."

Bud felt sad that he had disappointed his mother. He turned and ran all the way home. Main

Street was empty and there was no one on the public square. There was no one at home. Everyone was at Pierson's Grove.

Bud stood in the quiet kitchen. He wished this afternoon had never happened. He leaned on the wall behind the kitchen door. He thought about all the food on the picnic tables and everyone sitting about and eating. But he wasn't even hungry anymore. He sank down to the floor and just sat there.

After a very long time, as the sun set, the lonely kitchen was filled with the dark shadows of the coming night. Bud felt so sad as he thought about the torchlight parade, and he wondered who would carry his torch.

Suddenly, he heard heavy footsteps on the porch. He heard loud voices. Someone said, "Where's that boy? I want to see that boy!"

Bud held his breath. It was the speaker. He squeezed himself as tight as he could against the wall. Then he heard his mother.

"I think I can find him," she said. She went straight to the kitchen and took him by the hand and led him into the parlor.

"Young man!" roared Professor Clark. "Why aren't you marching in the torchlight parade?"

Bud hung his head.

"Speak up, my boy. Suppose we strike a bargain.

Bud felt too happy to speak.

I forgot my speech. You forgot your manners. Let's march in the parade together. What do you say?"

Bud couldn't believe his ears. Professor Clarke gave Bud his hand, and they hurried down to where the parade was lining up. Crowds of folks cheered and laughed as they came to the parade line. The visitor handed Bud his cane, and they strutted off together. Bud saw his friends watching him. Their mouths were hanging open in amazement.

"Hi, fellers" he called. Willie came on the run and gave Bud his torch. Father handed a torch to Professor Clarke, and the parade began.

Bud felt too happy to speak. The saxhorn band formed in front, and all the people fell in line behind. As far back as Bud could see there was a line of blazing lights. The ones farthest back looked like tiny stars.

It was the best Fourth of July Bud ever had. He never forgot the lesson he learned that day, though. When he mimicked someone, it was important that he make it clear that he was not making fun of that person.

Chapter 8

The National Road

Bud ran out the garden path, kicking his feet in front of him as he went around the house to the front gate. Climbing up on the gate he gently swung to and fro. He was still thinking about that glorious parade with all the torches flaming up into the darkness. He could still feel the excitement of holding his own torch high up in the air.

He looked up and down the National Road. He could see nearly down to Brandywine Creek to the east and almost to Black Swamp on the west. Just coming into view from the east was a long line of heavy wagons rolling along loaded with heavy logs from the forests. And he watched as they drove past his gate and on toward the Black Swamp. He wondered where they were going. And then he thought maybe to a sawmill in Indianapolis. The wagons were followed by a large herd of cattle with their hooves clattering on the plank road on their way to market. And then shortly behind the cattle were some men with two-wheeled carts loaded with corn and wheat on their way to the mill to be ground into flour. Bud loved to swing on his gate and watch all the traffic on the National Road, right in front of his house.

Upon the main street and the main highway
From East to West—historic in its day—
Known as the National Road. . . .

Then suddenly he saw what thrilled him most of all. He stood up and leaned over the gate to see as far as he could. He could hear the heavy rumbling of a huge wagon coming down the road. It was a Connestoga wagon hitched to four large horses. The wagon drove up and stopped right in front of Bud's house.

The neighborhood children all came running when they saw the "prairie schooner." They were all so excited. Willie called to the rest of their friends, "Look! Look! See, in front of Bud's house. There's a wagonload of travelers! Children, dogs, and everything!"

All the kids gathered around. Bud called to the children who were piling out of the wagon. "Come on over here and sit in the shade!" There were

The wagon drove up and stopped right in
front of Bud's house.

three boys and a little girl who hurried on over.
Bud opened the gate and started asking them all
kinds of questions. He had always wondered how it
would be to live and travel in a huge wagon.

"Do you get very tired traveling?" he asked.

"Yep, and we get tired of walking too," replied the biggest boy.

Bud was puzzled. "You don't have to walk if you don't want to, do you?"

"Yes, we do," the little girl nodded her head. "Sometimes we have to walk miles when the roads are muddy."

"Why?" asked Bud. He didn't understand.

"It's when the mud is so deep that the wagon bogs down and stops, then we have to walk," answered one of the other boys.

And the biggest boy continued, "Then Father helps us out of the wagon to lighten the load. Even then the horses can hardly pull their feet out of the mud."

"How do you get the wagon out, if the horses are stuck in the mud?" Bud asked.

"Well, one man keeps pulling the horses. The others lay big limbs of trees in front of the wheels. Then after a while, we finally get the wagon out and reach better roads again."

"Then do you all get back in the wagon?" Bud wanted to know. It didn't seem fair that the children would have to walk so long when they were so tired.

"Yes, but that isn't the worst thing," the older boy continued. "Sometimes there are horse thieves, and our men sit up all night with their guns across their knees. They do that to keep the robbers from stealing our horses and cattle. Sometimes the robbers prowl around our wagon all night, and nobody can sleep."

"You mean you stay awake all night listening for robbers!" Willie exclaimed.

"Yep." answered the older boy.

Bud shook his head. It sounded mighty exciting to travel in a prairie schooner. Maybe too exciting. Then he asked the children if they were thirsty, and he and Willie took them into the kitchen and gave each of them a nice cool drink of water and some cookies. Their father called to them that it was time to go. As the children climbed into the huge wagon, Bud and Willie waved good bye, and the wagon rolled on down the plank road and disappeared in the evening mist.

As soon as Father came home, Bud was so excited to tell him about his new friends traveling to the west in their prairie schooner. That evening the whole Riley family sat out of doors on the lawn in the moonlight. The neighborhood children joined them, and they all sat together on the cool green grass.

All the family and the boys' friends loved these summer evenings when Mr. Riley would tell them exciting stories of the early days on the National Road. This summer evening Reuben Riley told a story about the stagecoach and the Black Swamp.

The swamp was a stretch of dense, marshy woodland to the west of Greenfield.

"Years ago," Mr. Riley began, "the Black Swamp was a hiding place for bands of robbers. These robbers carried long pistols and knives in their belts. They would wait on horseback along the National road for a stagecoach loaded with passengers, mail, and goods to come by in the night.

"The old-time stagecoach was a long, four-wheeled closed carriage. People lived far apart and when they wanted to go a long way, they traveled by stagecoach. The driver sat on a high seat outside the carriage to drive the horses. There were usually two and sometimes three pairs of horses hitched to the stagecoach."

"We all liked to watch the stagecoaches come in," Mr. Riley said. "The driver blew a loud blast on his horn. He cracked his long whip. He galloped his horses into Greenfield, and swung them up to James B. Hart's Temperance Tavern, where he would pull them to a halt. Then he would call out in a loud voice, 'The United States Mail has arrived!'"

"Tell us about the Black Swamp," asked Bud. He could hardly wait for the next part. And the other boys said excitedly, "Tell us the story about the robbery!"

Mr. Riley then told them about Mr. James

Atherton. Mr. Atherton lived in a large, two-story house not far from the Black Swamp. One night a big storm blew up, and Mr. Atherton knew the road would be muddy and dangerous. He kept a candle burning in his room, and he sat up listening for the stagecoach to pass. He didn't like these stormy nights. He knew that the highwaymen did most of their robberies along the old road on nights like this. Long after midnight, the coach still hadn't come, and so the old man continued to wait, keeping his gun handy.

Presently he heard the rumbling of wheels and then a sound like a gunshot. He heard a terrible crash on the road below his house and the sound of trampling, frightened horses. He heard the panicked screams and shouts of the passengers.

Mr. Atherton reached for his gun and rushed out of the door. He fired into the ground. If there were robbers down on the road, he hoped the shot would frighten then away. Then he hurried down to the coach.

At the foot of the hill below his house he found the stagecoach, overturned. The six horses hitched to the coach were plunging and lurching as they tried to break loose from the heavy straps. The passengers said the coach had been attacked by robbers. Some of the people thought they had seen horsemen running away toward the Black Swamp. They thought Mr. Atherton's shot had scared them away.

Mr. Atherton took the frightened passengers to his house. Some were hurt, and others were only bruised and frightened. Mrs. Atherton used hot water and fresh linens to treat the injured. And then the Athertons provided hot coffee and food for everyone and made the people comfortable for the night. In the morning the large, clumsy stagecoach was repaired, and the passengers went safely on their way.

They will tell . . .
Of stage-coach days, highwaymen, and strange
*   crimes*
And yet unriddled mysteries of the times. . . .

Bud's eyes were wide as he waited for his father to finish the story. "Did they catch the robbers?" he asked.

Father smiled, "I don't think they did. . . . at least I never heard of it if they did."

Willie asked in wonder, "Do you think they are still in the Black Swamp?"

Johnty said, "Oh Willie, this was a long ago story. . . . The robbers are not still around here!"

And Father and Mother both laughed.

Chapter 9

The Black Swamp

When the days turned cool and the green leaves changed to scarlet and gold, the boys all had to go back to school. A week after Bud's birthday in 1859, their little brother Reuben Alexander Humboldt Riley was born. Bud thought it was a very grown-up name for such a little boy, but they always called him Hum. Johnty and Bud had fun playing with little Elva Mae and baby Hum, and Uncle Mart came often. Still the winter was long, and they looked forward to spring when school would be out.

At long last finally winter, and the tiring school days, came to an end. The boys leaped and shouted with joy when school was out, and they could run free again. Bud loved summertime and all the fun things the boys did like swimming in Brandywine creek, playing store, and putting on shows in the barn.

This warm summer day seemed much like every

other summer day in Greenfield. Little did Bud know that before the day was over, it would be different and unforgettable.

The boys were all busy getting ready for a show in Ed Howard's barn. Bud made a grand poster for the show with red and green letters, which said:

COMING SOON
A Big Show in Howard's Barn
New Scenery New Curtain
See Ed Howard's New Act

And he nailed it to the barn door.

The boys were practicing their acts. George Carr was going to sing an Irish song. Bud would turn flip-flops and play clown. Willie Pierson would imitate animals, and Ed Howard—well, nobody but Bud knew what Ed was going to do. He had been practicing secretly in the hayloft.

Bud was painting the new curtain because he was the only one who could do a really good job. Using a broad brush and colored whitewash, Bud was working on painting a scene in a forest with squirrels in the trees.

He was putting the finishing touches on the green trees when his father came to the barn door. "Bud," his father called. "I'm going to Indianapolis in the spring wagon, and I would like you to go along. Can you leave your work?"

Bud looked back at his curtain which was nearly finished, and the show wasn't going to be until tomorrow. "I'll be back later," he shouted to Ed and Willie. It was always exciting to go to town with his father, but he didn't know then just how exciting this trip was going to be.

He ran after his father and climbed up on the seat in the old spring wagon. Old Sorrel started off at a steady pace, as they rolled along on the plank road on their way to Indianapolis. The rhythmic sound of Sorrel's hooves clomping on the wooden road almost sounded like poetry.

When they reached the city, Father pulled the wagon up on Washington Street and carefully tied the reins to a hitching post. Mr. Riley had many errands to do, and he left Bud with the horse and wagon.

Bud liked to be alone in the wagon. He liked to watch the people and the buggies with their fine horses as they passed by. There were always so many things to see in the city.

Once in a while small streetcars hitched to two horses would pass. They were called "horsecars." The cars ran on a track laid in the center of the street. Old Sorrel didn't like these cars. He pranced about nervously whenever one passed.

Bud had just finished his lunch, which his father had brought with them, when a horsecar passed. As it did, the driver of the car gave a big gong a sharp, harsh ring. Sorrel jumped and pranced as if he wanted to run away. The whole wagon shook and rocked. Bud jumped down from the wagon and grabbed Sorrel's bridle and hung on, but it was a long time before the horse quieted down.

After that, Bud spent his time watching for streetcars. Whenever one came into sight, he climbed out of the wagon and held fast to Sorrel's head. He talked softly, "It's all right, Sorrel. Nothing's going to hurt you." Sorrel rolled his eyes and nuzzled Bud.

Bud watched the sun set. It looked as if it were going right down on the west end of Washington Street. The sky darkened as the sun dropped lower and lower and then disappeared. Bud wondered where his father was, when finally Reuben Riley came striding down the street. He was late, his business had kept him longer than he had expected. Both he and Bud were very tired.

"It's getting dark," Mr. Riley said. "I should have started earlier." He untied Sorrel, climbed up into the wagon, and started for home. He hurried the horse, and Sorrel, himself, was glad to trot along.

He wanted to get back to the safety of his own barn. Bud began to feel a little uneasy as he thought about the Black Swamp. He remembered the story his father had told about the highwaymen.

Just then three men came out of the shadows of the woods. The men stood in the middle of the road. Bud couldn't believe it.

He was frightened, and he held fast to his father's arm. Mr. Riley was a bit nervous himself. He said in a low voice, "Keep very quiet, Bud. Don't act as if you are scared. If there is any trouble, crawl under the seat."

The men stood right in the middle of the road. Mr. Riley was forced to stop. They looked rough and dangerous. One had a bloody bandage tied around his head, and he was staggering.

"Hello," said Mr. Riley in a calm, strong voice. "What can I do for you?" One of the men shook his head and seemed not to understand. He pointed first toward Greenfield, then to himself and the other two men. Then he pointed to the back of the wagon.

"Where are your horses?" asked Mr. Riley.

The man shook his head again and again went through the motions of wanting a ride. Mr. Riley was silent, as he tried to decide what to do. This made the man angry. He lunged at the wagon and tried to

Just then three men came out of the
shadows of the woods.

pull Mr. Riley down as he grabbed at the reins.

"No! No!" shouted Mr. Riley, as he clung to the
reins and pushed the man away from him. He
decided quickly that the safest way would be to

take them in the wagon. Without much trouble he made the man understand that he would take them, and they all climbed in.

Bud sat close to his father, stiff and straight. He felt as if he didn't dare move a muscle. He listened as the injured man moaned, and the other two talked excitedly to each other in a foreign language. One time the man who seemed to be the leader leaned forward and began talking to Mr. Riley, but he couldn't understand what he was saying.

As they came into Greenfield by the Black Swamp, the large man laid a heavy hand on Mr. Riley's shoulder. He pulled the reins, and Sorrel stopped. Two of the men climbed out and carefully lifted the injured man to his feet. Without a word, they all disappeared into the shadows of the night.

Without waiting to even look back, Reuben Riley drove home as fast as he could. Bud heaved a sigh. He felt like he could finally breathe.

Quietly, Father said, "Bud, we won't say anything about this tonight. We don't want anyone to worry."

Chapter 10

Barn Show

When Bud woke up, he couldn't believe the frightening experience that he and Father had last night. It was unreal, like a bad dream. But when he ran downstairs, Father was telling Mother about the strange men, and he knew it was true. As soon as he had bolted down his breakfast, he ran down to the Howard's barn to tell all the boys.

He was breathless as he told them the thrilling story of the night on the road by the Black Swamp. Ed said, "I bet that injured man had been shot!" and Willie added, "I bet they were highwaymen." Johnty said, "You and Father were lucky that they didn't shoot you!"

Bud nodded, but he did say that he didn't think they had guns.

Noey Bixler said, "I think there'll be some officers of the law coming to Greenfield any minute to get them."

But Willie interrupted, "Where do you suppose they are now?"

"Do you suppose they are still hiding in the Black Swamp?" Johnty asked fearfully. And the boys all looked at one another with wide eyes as they wondered where those three men could be lurking.

Later in the day, Dr. Edwards saw Mr. Riley, and said "Riley, I had a strange experience last night. Long after I had gone to bed, a rough-looking man came to my door. He spoke a language I didn't understand, but he finally made it clear that he and his two friends had been in a runaway wagon. Their horse was gone, and their wagon was broken. The worst of it was that one of the men was hurt. The man wanted me to see his friend. I went and found the man was indeed badly injured, but I patched him up as best I could. They all left in the direction of the Black Swamp. The injured man was almost carried by his friends. I hope they found their horse."

With all the excitement, it was difficult for the boys to get back to their preparations for their show, but the sign was up, the curtain was painted, the stage set, and the seats were ready for the spectators.

Wasn't it a good time,
Long Time Ago—
When we all were little tads
And first played 'Show!'

On the day of the show, most of the boys ran home for lunch. Bud and George stayed behind to watch Ed practice his secret act one more time. Ed's secret act was supposed to be a backward somersault. He did his cartwheels and his handsprings, then with a running spring Ed made a half turn, and fell with a thud that shook the stage.

The boys waited for him to try again, but Ed lay still. Something had gone wrong. Bud brought a cup of water and threw it in Ed's face. Ed opened his eyes and moaned, but he didn't move! The boys were worried, but they didn't want to take him home. They were afraid their parents would stop the show.

Bud thought about Dr. Howard's carriage in the shed next to the barn. Its soft cushions would be just the place for Ed. Bud and George carried Ed into the shed and placed him in the carriage. Ed had stopped moaning, and his eyes were open. The fall had knocked the breath out of him, but the boys hoped he would be able to do his act in a little while.

Soon the hour for the show drew near. The performers got dressed for their acts. George Carr sold tickets and told about the wonderful things to be seen in the show. Bud went outside and turned flip-flops. He said funny things to make the crowd want to come and see the show.

The village children came in crowds, both boys and girls. They paid George Carr the usual jelly biscuits or eggs for their tickets, went in quickly, and the big show began.

After each act Bud went to see how Ed was getting along, but Ed was afraid to try his secret act. When the show was nearly half over, the crowd started to get restless. They shouted, "Bring out Ed Howard, or we'll go home!"

Even Bud's songs and dances failed to hold them. Finally, when Ed didn't appear, the audience slowly drifted away. The great new barn show was over. Bud walked slowly into the buggy shed. He was so disappointed and a little angry with Ed for letting the show down. None of their shows had ever failed before. He tried to think of some way to get the audience to come back.

And then he had an idea. He would turn the show into a stagecoach robbery! The carriage would be the stagecoach. Ed would be a captured victim. He wouldn't have to move because he would

The village children . . . went in quickly and
the big show began.

be bound and gagged. Bud would be a victim, too. George, Noey, and the rest of the boys could be the highwaymen robbers.

He thought about the costumes and decided that all he and Ed would need was red grease paint on their faces to look like they were injured, and the highwayman could tie kerchiefs over their faces for their disguises. He ran into the barn where they had the make-up for the show and got some red grease paint. After he painted Ed's face and smeared paint on his own face, he sat down to rest a moment before he went to get the other boys.

The shed was dark and cool, the soft cushions of the carriage were comfortable and the boys were tired. In a moment both boys fell asleep. They slept through the afternoon.

Suppertime came, and Ed and Bud were still asleep. No one had seen the boys since the show. Their parents became worried and started to look for them.

Dr. Howard, followed by some of the children in the neighborhood, went directly to his buggy shed to get his carriage to look for Ed and Bud. He threw open the doors, and the light from the setting sun shone in.

There lay the sleeping victims, Bud and Ed. Their faces looked as if they were covered with blood, because the paint had run down their cheeks. One little girl shrieked with fright when she saw them.

Her scream awakened the boys, and they sat up startled by the noise. Bud jumped down from the carriage, and Ed, who had completely recovered, came right behind him!

When the children saw that the boys were not hurt, they started shouting, "When do we get to see the rest of the show?"

Bud had to laugh to himself about his plans for the great stagecoach robbery act, which never happened. Bud looked at Ed, and Ed looked at Bud. Together they said, "The barn show is over for today!"

Chapter 11

Circus Day Parade

It was just after the Noted Traveler's visit that the Circus came to town.

The Noted Traveler came on a special Saturday afternoon, and he and Father both gave speeches down by the Courthouse. Bud was always proud of Father, the way that he stood straight and tall and spoke so well. Bud thought to himself that he would never be as good a speaker as Father.

That evening after dinner, they all sat around the parlor and talked and laughed and had such a good time. Little Elva May said a verse, and Bud recited a poem. And they all laughed at baby Hum as he talked in his own baby talk.

But when the Noted Traveler started to talk, Mother and Father both became very serious. He talked about the terrible times with slavery in the South. He told about how slaves were trying to escape and were going through Indiana on their way to freedom in Canada. He said that they were going on the "Underground Railway."

Bud's eyebrows drew down as he tried to imagine how frightening it would be to be all alone and trying to run away. His blue eyes filled with tears. His Mother put her arm around him. He was embarrassed when he saw his father's frown.

The Noted Traveler continued to talk as he described how the Underground Railway worked. It was not really a railroad, but a number of people who helped the runaway slaves, by hiding them in their homes. These were called stations, and then by dark of night they loaded the escaping slaves into wagons and took them on to the next safe house, or station, along the way.

Father was very thoughtful for days after the visit of the Noted Traveler. Bud noticed that Mother and Father talked quietly with each other, and when Grandmother came over they all talked so seriously. Father had always belonged to the Democratic Party until he had become so concerned about the state of the Union over the issue of slavery. After much discussion and thought, he had joined the newly-founded Republican Party in the presidential election of 1856. Bud didn't understand all of this, but it seemed to be very important to his father.

Only a few days after the serious visit of the

Noted Traveler, Bud's mood changed when the circus came to town. The August day was very hot, but the whole town turned out to see the festive circus parade. Circuses came to town almost every year, but this was the best circus ever.

The grand white and gold bandwagon, drawn by huge, sleek horses prancing along, shone in the bright sunlight. The bandmen in their fine uniforms strutted proudly down the road. The bugles played and played to the rhythm of the tenor drummer's beat! Then came the horsemen, two by two, with their colorful feathery plumes waving in the breeze.

A huge elephant came ambling down the street with a little pony dancing at his side.

"Look at that cute little pony!" Bud shouted.

"Oh, and the camels! Look at the camels!" yelled Willie as the camels, with their big eyes and eyelashes, followed in line.

Big barred cages jolted along slowly with their rare and exotic animals—lions and tigers and monkeys, and maybe a dancing bear. Last of all came the clowns making merry and shaking hands with the children along the way.

"Oh, the Circus Day Parade! How the bugles
played and played!

And how the glossy horses tossed their flossy
manes and neighed,
As the rattle and rhyme of the tenor-
drummer's time
Filled all the hungry hearts of us with
melody Sublime!

The marvelous Rensen and Lake Circus had an exciting animal show. Best of all it gave a night performance, burning lard oil for lights. The band played on and on, as the ringmaster went through the animal acts cracking his whip masterfully.

Bud and Johnty and all their friends went wild with delight. They had never seen such an exciting show. The antics of a cage full of monkeys had them rolling with laughter.

No longer were Bud and his friends satisfied with their barn shows. The time had come for them to have a circus show. So the day after the circus left town, the boys got together to plan their own circus show.

"We can have our circus in the dirt ring where the real circus had its show!" Bud said enthusiastically.

"And we can have all our animals in our circus!" Willie added.

The Rensen and Lake Circus had trained animals. The village boys had trained animals, too. Willie Pierson had a pet fawn, which he had trained to follow him and hunt for sugar in his pocket. Noey Bixler had many animals—wild racoons, foxes, hawks, and owls, which he had captured and tamed.

Noey had given Bud a flying squirrel. Bud spent hours training her for the show. He called her the Flying Lady, and she became very tame as they trained her to fly from post to post. But before the circus show, she accidentally suffocated as she slept with Bud in his bed. Bud had been devastated with grief, and he had cried and cried.

Though Bud was so sad about the Flying Lady, they still had to get ready for the show. Bud and his friends did not need to do much rehearsing because they had lots of experience in giving their shows. Bud could perform on a bar. He was good at turning handsprings. Sometimes he would turn handsprings and cartwheels all the way down the walk when he was doing errands for his mother.

Bud was also the ringmaster of the circus. As the boys rehearsed for the show, they tried to copy the acts of the big show, and they copied the costumes of the performers as best they could.

"We need music, too," announced Ed. "The real

circus had band music, and we need to have a band also!" They decided that Johnty would play his flute, and Johnnie Mitchell would play his drum.

Noey Bixler had the hardest job and the best. He had to perform with the menagerie of animals in the ring. Since Bud's flying squirrel had died, Willie Pierson's pet fawn had to take its place.

They got several little puppies and put them in a cage. Next to the puppies' cage they placed another cage full of little kittens. Bud made a sign that said, "Monkeys," and the little children laughed and giggled as they watched the puppies and kittens, even if they weren't real monkeys.

The main animal act was a wild lion, which was really Noey's dog Shep. Shep was a beautiful shepherd dog with long thick fur. Noey sheared off all Shep's fur, except for the long hair on Shep's head and the tip of his tail. Noey brushed this fur straight up to make him look more fierce and dangerous. Then he painted black rings around Shep's eyes to make him look mean and wicked. After Noey finished with him, Shep was so ashamed of himself that he hung his head and let his tail droop straight down.

Though when it came time for Shep to perform in the ring with Noey, his head and tail went up. He looked very wild as he tumbled and rolled over

Noey Bixler had to perform with the
menagerie of animals in the ring.

and over with Noey. He growled fiercely, showing his teeth and pretending to bite Noey.

Every child in the village came to the circus, and they paid lots of pins, jelly biscuits and eggs in exchange for seats. Everybody was happy.

As they started home, Bud said, "Noey, your old Shep dog was the best act in the show."

"Yes," Noey answered soberly. "He was pretty good. But I wonder how I'm going to get the paint off his face."

"I guess Shep will just have to be a lion till it wears off." Bud answered.

Chapter 12

War Between the States

Bud's teacher at school said that she thought he was too old to be called Bud, and that he should be called by his proper name, which was Jim. So from that time on, he was called Jim.

This was the year 1860, and Reuben Riley had been selected to be a delegate-at-large for the Republican Convention to be held in Chicago.

Jim and Johnty went down to the train station to see Father off. Mr. Riley swung up on the train car and waved good-bye. The boys stood and waved as the train rolled slowly down the track.

Silently they walked along together, when Jim looked up and realized they were almost at Grandma Riley's. Both boys started to run and ran up the front steps and in the front door.

"My land," Grandma cried, "I'm glad you're here! I was just starting to fry some apples."

Jim and Johnty sat at the kitchen table and

watched their grandmother frying the apples in her skillet on the stove. The apples smelled so good, and there was a cheery sound of the sputtering of the apples as they cooked.

"Your father got off on the train all right?" Grandmother asked.

Jim nodded, "But I don't quite understand what he is going to do in Chicago."

Grandma set their plates of apples in front of them, sat down at the table, and started to talk. Jim listened carefully. Grandma Riley knew almost everything. She explained how the delegates at the Republican convention were going to select a candidate for the president of the United States. Then in November there would be the presidential election, and the President would be elected.

Grandma Riley smiled, and she lifted her chin a bit as she said, "I am very proud that your father was selected to help nominate the presidential candidate for the Republican Party!"

Father was gone for several days, and when he came home, the boys were asleep in their beds. It was the middle of the night when Reuben Riley burst into the room where the children were sleeping. He had a lamp in his hand, which lit up the room and awakened the children. Jim and Johnty and Elva May and even little Hum ran down to the parlor and gathered around their father. Mother leaned forward in her chair, and they all listened with excitement as he told them about the convention in Chicago.

Father's dark eyes were shining as he announced proudly, "We have nominated Abraham Lincoln to be the Republican candidate for president! The events were thrilling, as the West was victorious in choosing Lincoln over Seward from the East!"

Abraham Lincoln was elected president of the United States in 1860, and was inaugurated on March 4th, 1861. On April 12th, 1861, the Confederate Artillery opened fire on Fort Sumter in the harbor of Charleston, South Carolina, and the War Between the States had begun.

Immediately Reuben Riley volunteered to serve in the Army for ninety days. He reassured Mrs. Riley and the children that he would be back home very soon. But he was wrong. He did return, but only to sign up again.

Everything happened so quickly. Jim had trouble understanding. He could not believe that their father was going off to war. One morning Jim thought he heard a drum and fife corps, but then he wondered if he were dreaming. Jim sat straight up in bed, and then he ran to the window. He could hear men marching, and as he looked out, he saw his father and neighbor men and boys drilling like soldiers in the street.

He dressed quickly and ran outdoors. The women stood watching. Some were crying. Mother didn't cry. She looked proud, but she looked sad, too.

"It is war," said his mother. "There is civil war, and your father is going to fight to save the Union."

Every morning Jim awakened to the sound of the drums and fifes. Father was made captain of the company, and every morning the company of men drilled up and down Main Street.

One morning, everything was quiet. Jim ran to the Courthouse Square. The men were lined up ready to march, with Father at the head of the company. A brand new flag waved over the men's heads. Mother and Mrs. Permelia Thayer and some of the other women in the neighborhood had made the flag.

Captain Reuben Riley gave the signal. The fife sounded its mournful tune, and the drum rolled with a regular beat, and the line began to march. Down the road the company went led by the old saxhorn band. This time they didn't turn back. They all went on and on. Jim stood in the middle of the road. He felt such an emptiness in his chest. He watched the column of men march away and fade

Down the road the company went. . . .

in the dust of the old road. The flag waved a last good-bye.

Old Glory! Say, who,
By the ships and the crew,
And the long, blended ranks of the gray and
the blue—
Who gave you, Old Glory, the name that you,
Bear . . .
Who gave you the name of Old Glory? Say,
Who—Who gave you the name of Old Glory?

Chapter 13

Little Orphant Annie

Everything was different in the Riley home after Father had gone off to war. The pay for the soldiers was very little, and oftentimes did not arrive. Mother stretched their food so everyone would have enough to eat. They wore their old clothes, mended again and again. There was a feeling of sadness in the air as everyone worried about the soldiers off at war.

Mother worked with all the other women at the Soldiers' Aid Society. They made bandages, socks, and packets of scraped lint. The lint was used on soldiers' wounds. It was the only way they knew to stop bleeding in those days.

Jim felt like the whole world was gray and grim. There was no time for shows and circuses. Noey Bixler and most of the other older boys had gone off to war with Father's company. Lee Harris, the school teacher who roomed at Grandma Riley's house, had gone too.

Jim and Johnty did whatever they could do to help. They helped with the work at home and ran errands for everybody. They met all the trains that passed through the town. The trains were full of soldiers, some going to war, and some coming home sick and wounded. The boys gave them milk and cookies and filled their canteens with water.

One cold, bleak winter day, a cart drew up in front of the house, and a man and a little girl came to the door. As Mother opened the door, the bitterly cold wind blew through into the hall. She motioned for the man and the little girl to step inside.

Quickly she closed the door behind them. The man took off his hat and started to talk. "This is Mary Alice, and I'm her uncle." He hesitated for just a moment as if it were difficult for him to continue. He swallowed hard and then said, "I'm wondering if you could give her a home. She would be glad to help you out for her board and keep."

Mary Alice was a strange little girl. She was about twelve years old. Though the winter was cold, she wore a very light shawl over a plain black dress, and a summer straw hat perched sideways on her head. She was very thin, and her eyes were bright with fear. She shivered as she stood in the doorway.

Her uncle explained that she had no parents, and he had tried to take care of her, but that he had fallen on hard times and couldn't help her. He wondered if Mrs. Riley could take her in.

Gentle, kind Mrs. Riley said, "Of course, she can stay." And she showed her into the kitchen as the man closed the door and left.

Mary Alice walked into the room slowly. Her eyes were wide in her pale face as she looked at the children seated around the table. Jim and Johnty got to their feet to stand and offer her a chair. She was about Jim's age, but she was so small she looked much younger. Jim thought he had never seen a girl who looked so scared. He smiled and so did Johnty and Elva May. Even little Hum smiled at her. Slowly Mary Alice smiled, too.

Mary Alice seemed very happy in the Riley's home. Mrs. Riley wondered at her cheerfulness. She worked from morning to night. She didn't stop until all the dishes were washed and dried, and the last task was finished.

All the children helped with the work, but Mary Alice had a special way about her. She turned each task into play. When she fed the chickens, she pretended she was a grand princess throwing gifts to her people. When she carried the dishes to the cupboard, she stepped as if she were marching to music. She talked to herself when she was alone and liked to imagine she was talking to many people.

She loved the curving hall stairs, and after their work was done, the children would get together in the front hall. Mary Alice named each step, and she told them that all sorts of fairies, imps, and gnomes lived underneath the stairs.

"What are they doing there?" asked Elva May.

"Oh, I don't know exactly. Maybe they moved in to keep warm," she said.

"Are there any goblins under the steps?" Elva May asked again.

"Goblins are pretty dangerous, aren't they, Mary Alice?" asked Jim.

"Not if you behave yourself and mind your mother and father," was Mary Alice's answer. "But the gobble-uns'll git you if you don't watch out!"

Mary Alice walked up the stairs very slowly, pausing on each step. When she reached the top, she called in an eerie voice, "Mary Alice! Mary Alice!" and her voice trailed off as she said, "Oh, she has gone home. . . ."

Jim and the other children stood at the foot of the stairs just looking at each other, as Mary Alice disappeared upstairs. Elva Mae clutched at Jim as she shivered.

At night before they went to bed and all the work was done, Mary Alice would tell her strange, make-believe stories. They all sat on the floor in

At night before they went to bed . . . Mary Alice
would tell her strange make-believe stories.

front of the fireplace. The dim light of the candles
made strange shadows on the wall, and the hissing
of the fire made a lonely sound. She told such
weird and frightening stories that Elva May and
Hum were afraid to go to bed after her tales, and
even Jim felt a little uneasy about how true her
stories might be.

Mary Alice stayed in the Riley home until summer. Then early one morning, while the Riley family was still asleep, her uncle came in his farm cart
and took her away.

The strange stories she had told made the

children wonder what had really happened to Mary Alice. Elva May asked Jim if he thought the goblins had come and taken her away. He shook his head. He didn't really know, but her sad cry "Oh, she has gone home . . ." kept echoing in his thoughts.

Many years later, when he was a man, Jim Riley wrote a poem about Mary Alice Smith. He didn't call her by her real name. He called her "Little Orphant Annie." He ended the poem the way Mary Alice always ended her weird, make-believe tales and stories:

An' little orphant Annie says, when the blaze is blue,
An' the lamp-wick sputters, an' the wind goes woo-oo!
An' you hear the crickets quit, an' the moon is gray,
An' the lightnin'-bugs in dew is all squenched away,—
You better mind yer parunts, an' yer teachers fond an'dear,
An' churish them 'at loves you, an' dry the orphant's tear,
An' he'p the pore an' needy ones 'at clusters all about,

Er the Gobble-uns'll git you
  Ef you
       Don't
            Watch
                 Out!

Chapter 14

Grandmother's Secret

With so many of the men and big boys away at the war, everyone at home had to work very hard. Johnty worked in the fields at the farm. Elva May helped mother in the house, and Jim took care of old Sorrel, carried in the wood, and worked in the garden.

The sweat ran down Jim's face as he hoed row after row. He stopped for a moment to take off his old straw hat and wipe his forehead on his shirt-sleeve. He looked down the road, hoping to see Uncle Martin. But instead he saw some soldiers in shabby uniforms walking along slowly. They waved back as Jim waved to them. He wondered whether they had been injured in battle. There were such sad things to see on the road now. By night, sometimes there were soldiers who had deserted and were running away from the war. They hid by the roadside during the day and slipped through the town in the dark of night.

Jim swung his hoe until dusk began to fall. Wearily, he put his tools in the barn and went into the house, calling to his mother, "Has Uncle Mart come yet?"

Mother smiled gently. She knew how much Jim looked forward to Martin's visits. Though Martin worked as a printer in Indianapolis, he visited often. "I haven't seen him, Jim. Perhaps he went to Grandma's house first."

Johnty came in just then from doing his chores out on the farm and said, "I think he is at Grandma's. Let's go over and see!"

They ran up on Grandmother's porch and found it strange that the front door was closed on such a warm summer evening. Jim knocked, and it seemed a very long time until Martin opened the door but only a crack.

"Uncle Mart!" exclaimed Jim.

Martin barely poked his head out to say, "I'll be over in a few minutes," and then started to close the door.

"Wait a minute," Johnty said quickly, "Can't we come in?"

Martin looked behind him as Grandma spoke up, "Let them come in, Martin."

Jim and Johnty exchanged glances. They couldn't

There was a Confederate soldier . . .
sitting at the kitchen table.

understand what was going on. Slowly they walked
into the house, and they were shocked at what they
saw!

There was a Confederate soldier, in a shabby
butternut colored uniform, sitting at the kitchen
table. His eyes were bleary, and his bearded face
was pale and thin.

Jim and Johnty couldn't believe their eyes that
their grandmother had a Confederate soldier in

her kitchen! That she was hiding an enemy soldier. Johnty was especially irate. He felt strongly that any Confederate soldier was a rebel and should be shot.

"He needs to be turned in!" Johnty shouted.

Uncle Martin said quietly, "Johnty, just calm down."

"But this is illegal, how can Grandma hide this rebel?" He glared at his grandmother.

Grandma closed her eyes and took a deep breath, as she began, "Jim and Johnty, you know I would not do anything wrong." She turned toward the man at the table, who was sitting with his head on his hands. "This man is my oldest son, John," and then she repeated softly, "your Uncle John."

Uncle Martin pulled out kitchen chairs and motioned for the boys to sit down, as Grandma went on. "He has lived in the South for many years. When the war broke out, he went into the Confederate Army. He was captured and has been in a prison camp in Illinois. He escaped and is trying to get back home. He is sick and wounded. We need to hide him here until he is able to go on." She looked directly at Jim and Johnty and asked, "Will you help me?"

Martin interrupted to ask, "Would you have him incarcerated?"

Johnty frowned as he demanded, "Have him what?"

Jim knew how Uncle Martin liked big words. And he said, "Have him put in jail."

Martin looked straight at Johnty, "Would you have your own uncle in the gloomy dungeons of jail?"

Jim thought about how good Grandma Riley always was to them and that Uncle John was her son just like their father and Uncle Mart. They couldn't let her down. He looked at Johnty as he spoke for both of them. "Of course, we will help you!" Johnty didn't say anything, but he didn't disagree.

They kept their secret well. As soon as Uncle John was strong enough, he left. He was afraid he might bring harm to Grandmother Riley. He didn't go back to his army post. He was too ill, but he did get safely home. Only when the war was over did anyone know that he had been in Greenfield.

The war years stretched out. Father was able to come home on leave, and then after he suffered wounds and injuries he spent time at home as he recuperated. He finally came home to stay in September of 1864 after being away at war for three and a half years.

Jim was fifteen years old when word flew from house to house that the war was finally over. Every day after that, the woman and boys went to the edge of the town and watched the road. Each time a cloud of dust appeared, they asked, "Are they coming? Are the men coming?" Each time they were disappointed.

One beautiful day Jim went far down the road to look. It was so clear he could see a very long way. Far toward the west, he thought he saw a speck. The speck grew. A cloud of dust was following it. He waited, and finally, he was sure. A troop of soldiers was approaching, led by the old saxhorn band. The men were coming home!

He ran home to tell his mother, and she ran to tell their neighbors. Jim never forgot that day. How proud he was of his father when he stood on the Courthouse steps and spoke to the people. The band played and the women laughed and cried. Mother lifted Jim's baby sister Mary Elizabeth, who had been born during the war, high over her head so that she could see Father.

Then the crowd began to shout, "Give us a poem before we go home, Jim." Jim recited one of their favorite war poems. "Another! Give us another poem," they shouted again and again.

Everyone was so happy and having such a good time. Finally, Jim began to mimic people, just as he had when he was a small boy. He made them laugh and laugh, and the band played one more tune.

Chapter 15

The Medicine Show

After the war, times were hard for the Riley family. When Reuben Riley returned to Greenfield after the war, he had to start his law practice all over again. The Riley family moved in with Grandma Riley in her little house because they had to sell their house on the National Road. As they walked away from their white house with the green shutters, Jim said, "I promise . . . someday I will buy it back and we can all live here again!"

Reuben Riley looked at Jim sadly. It didn't seem likely.

Johnty went to work to help the family out, but since Jim was only sixteen, he needed to keep going to school. After classes were over, he often went to the shoeshop of Tom Snow. Tom Snow was an Englishman who had come to America to live. He loved to read, and shelves of books lined the walls of his shop. In one corner sat a table with a checkerboard. The young men of Greenfield gathered here to discuss books and the happenings of the world.

One day, Mr. Riley called Jim to his office and said, "Jim, you will be finishing school soon. Have you given any thought to what you would like to be? Would you like to study law?"

Jim knew that his father wanted him to study law. He hesitated for only a moment, and then he answered, "No, Father . . . I don't want to be a lawyer."

His father's face looked stern, "Then what do you want to be?"

Jim answered, "I don't know."

Jim continued in school. Lee Harris, his teacher, led Jim to read many good books and encouraged him to write his poems. Then in 1870 Jim's mother died. Jim felt such despair. He didn't know how he could get along without his mother.

Jim knew he could no longer be a schoolboy. He had to start making a living. For a while he was a salesman in a nearby town. Then one day he returned to Greenfield. "I've decided what I would like to do," Jim said to his father. "I would like to be a painter."

Mr. Riley bought him some paint and brushes, and Jim Riley started to paint houses and signs

Most of the people of the village crowded around Doctor
McCrillus' medicine wagon.

around town. He didn't stop writing poems,
though. Many of the signs he put up were written
in rhyme. Jim's poems started to appear in the
Greenfield paper. One of them was even printed in

an Indianapolis newspaper.

One bright morning in 1872 a medicine show came into Greenfield in a wagon driven by a team of beautiful horses. The wagon was brightly decorated with signs announcing "Doctor S. B. McCrillus—

Medicine Man." The wagon rolled down the National Road and stopped in the public square.

Jim had just finished painting a sign for the general store on the corner of the square. When he saw the gaudy, painted wagon, he went over to it and read all the signs. He thought about how exciting it would be to travel from town to town and give shows to all the people gathered around.

Throughout the day signs for the show began to appear all over town.

That night Jim and his friends went to the town square to see the show. Most of the people of the village crowded around Doctor McCrillus' medicine wagon. The show took place at the back of the wagon. Oil torches around the wagon lit up the stage. On the stage on the back of the wagon were stands with many jars and colorful bottles.

First on the program a young man played some music on a French harp, and then there was some singing and a few skits. Finally, Doctor McCrillus, the medicine man, appeared. He was a huge man with a red face and long white whiskers. He wore a long-tailed coat and a brightly colored vest.

"Ladies and Gentlemen," he began. In his booming voice, he told about his medicines. He waved his arms as he described the wondrous cures of his miraculous remedies.

Jim watched it all, his eyes wide with excitement. "What a wonderful speaker," he thought. "This is what I would like to do. I want to travel with the medicine show."

After the show was over, Jim stayed to see Doctor McCrillus as he was selling his bottles and jars of medicines. When most of the crowd had gone, Jim went up to the medicine wagon and stood before Doctor McCrillus.

"Sir," said Jim, "do you need a sign painter?"

"Why, I already have one, young man," said Doctor McCrillus.

"I'm a good sign painter," said Jim. "Did you see the signs on the way into town? I painted them. Besides, I can play the guitar a little."

"Hm-m," said the medicine man. "I could use another sign painter. You say you play the guitar?" He thought for a moment, and then he said, "You're hired! Be ready to leave early in the morning."

Jim could hardly wait until the next day. His dreams of joining the travelers on the National Road were to come true at last.

When dawn broke, Mr. Riley waved to the bright wagon as it rolled out of town. On the high front seat sat Jim. His pale hair was shining in the early morning sun. On his freckled face was a wonderful smile.

James Whitcomb Riley was often called
the "Children's Poet."

Jim worked for Doctor McCrillus for about a
year, but then he returned to Greenfield, where he
took up his sign painting business again. Jim

began to give readings of his poems, and he kept writing his poetry. One of his poems was published in New York.

For a short time, Jim traveled with another medicine show. He took a job as a reporter with a newspaper in Anderson, Indiana, and wrote advertisements, but he continued writing his poetry.

After a short while he returned home to Greenfield. His poems were now being published in newspapers around the country, and he was being asked to read his poetry in programs in neighboring towns.

In 1883, James Whitcomb Riley's first book of poems was published. It was called *The Old Swimmin'-Hole and 'Leven More Poems*. Much of James Whitcomb Riley's poetry was based on his own childhood in Greenfield, Indiana. He wrote with an understanding and love for children and was often called the "Children's Poet."

The End

What Happened Next?

• James Whitcomb Riley's first book of poetry, *The Old Swimmin' Hole and 'Leven More Poems,* was published in 1883. The popularity of his poems grew due to his lectures and readings across the United States.

• By the end of the 19th century, James Whitcomb Riley was one of the most recognized figures in the United States.

• In 1915, the poet's birthday was celebrated nationwide—more than a million school children honored Mr. Riley.

• James Whitcomb Riley died in Indianapolis, Indiana in 1916. His homes in Indianapolis and Greenfield, Indiana are museums open for touring.

For more information about James Whitcomb Riley, visit the Patria Press website at www.patriapress.com

Fun Facts About
James Whitcomb Riley*

* James Whitcomb Riley was called the "Hoosier Poet." "Hoosier Poet" became a brand name for canned fruits, vegetables and coffee.

* Before he became a famous poet, Mr. Riley worked as a shoe clerk, a house painter, a door-to-door Bible salesman and a sign painter.

* James Whitcomb Riley counted among his friends Mark Twain, Lew Wallace, author of *Ben-Hur;* President Benjamin Harrison and Eugene V. Debs, founder of the American Socialist Party.

* Riley Hospital for Children, named for the poet, opened in Indianapolis, Indiana in 1924 and is the only hospital in Indiana that provides care exclusively to children.

*Many thanks to Elizabeth Van Allen, author of *James Whitcomb Riley, A Life,* (Bloomington: Indiana University Press, 1999) for permission to use source material in her book for the creation of "Fun Facts About James Whitcomb Riley."

About the Authors

Minnie Belle Mitchell was born in 1863 and lived in Greenfield, Indiana, near where James Whitcomb Riley grew up. *James Whitcomb Riley, Hoosier Poet* (original title) first published in 1942, was her only book, which she wrote for the original Childhood of Famous Americans Series®.

Co-author Montrew Dunham, a third generation Hoosier, was born and reared in Indianapolis, Indiana and grew up reading and reciting the poetry of James Whitcomb Riley. She attended elementary school in Indianapolis at a time when Indiana schoolchildren were contributing their quarters toward the Riley Museum Home of Lockerbie Street.

Mrs. Dunham received her A.B. degree from Butler University and her M.A. from Northwestern University. She has authored numerous biographies for children, including *Oliver Wendell Holmes: Boy of Justice, George Westinghouse: Young Inventor, Anne Bradstreet: Young Puritan Poet, Abner Doubleday: Young Baseball Pioneer, Mahalia Jackson: Young Gospel Singer, John Muir: Young Naturalist, Langston Hughes: Young Black Poet, Margaret Bourke: Young Photographer, Roberto Clemente: Young Ballplayer, Neil Armstrong: Young Flyer, Thurgood Marshall: Young Justice,* and *Ronald Reagan: Young Leader.*